D1561625

Leaning Forward

for Rabbi Sanford Saperstein & Leah Saperstein

Grace Paley
Jan 18 1986

Leaning
Forward

poems by

Grace
Paley

Afterword by Jane Cooper

GRANITE PRESS
PENOBSCOT
MAINE

Poems Copyright © 1985 by Grace Paley
Afterword Copyright © 1985 by Jane Cooper

First Printing: Letterpress limited edition of 125 copies,
August–September 1985.
Second Printing: Paperback trade edition of 5000 copies,
September 1985.
All rights reserved.

Set in Monotype Bell by Michael Bixler
Printed at Furbush-Roberts, Bangor, Maine
Photography: Margot Balboni
Design: Bea Gates
Logo: Adrienne Weiss/ Bea Gates

ISBN 0-9614886-0-3
Library of Congress #85-080552

Published by GRANITE PRESS
BOX 7, PENOBSCOT, MAINE 04476

ACKNOWLEDGMENTS

Publication of this book has been funded, in part, by a grant from the Maine State Commission on the Arts and Humanities and the Maine Writers & Publishers Small Press Assistance Project.

Poems in this collection were first published, some in slightly different versions, in the following magazines: *"Chelsea"*, *"Field"*, *"Ikon"*, *"Persea"*, *"Shankpainter"*, *"Sunbury"*, *"Win Magazine"*.

"One day when I was a child long ago" and *"This is about the women of that country"* were included in NO MORE MASKS!: AN ANTHOLOGY OF POEMS BY WOMEN, Ed. Florence Howe and Ellen Bass, Anchor Press/ Doubleday Anchor Books, Garden City, New York, 1973.

"One day lying on my stomach" was first published in FATHERS, REFLECTIONS BY DAUGHTERS, Ed. Ursula Owens, Virago Press Ltd., London, 1983 and published in the United States by Pantheon Books, a division of Random House, Inc., New York in 1985 under the same title.

"What would happen" was issued as a broadside in a letterpress limited edition under the title, *"Goldenrod"*, Granite Press, Penobscot, Maine, 1983.

The publisher extends thanks to the following people for their support & intelligent advice during this time of change for the press: Michaela Baldwin, Nancy Bereano, Christi Cassidy, Leslie Chatterton, Jane Cooper, Eva Kollisch , Rosa Lane, Joan Larkin, Jon Leach & Nancy Nowak, Roz Parr, Martha Ramsey, Elaine Summers, Zoe Weinstein, Adrienne Weiss and Grace Paley.

CONTENTS

I   *A woman invented fire*   15
Stanzas: Old Age and the Conventions of Retirement
     Have Driven My Friends from the Work They Love   16
One Day when I was a child   long ago   18
Drowning (I)   19
Drowning (II)   20
The women let the tide go out   21
A Warning   22
The veins that stand   23
At the Battery   24
20th Street   Spring   25
note to grandparents   26
psalm   27
Mulberry Street ends in good works   28
The boys from St. Bernard's   29
Children walking with their grandmothers   30
On the Fourth Floor   31
Middle Age Poem   32
On Mother's Day   33
Having Arrived by Bike at Battery Park   35

II   *A stranger calling a dog*   38
on certain days I am not in love   39
One day   lying on my stomach   41
Some days I am lonesome   42
I cannot keep my mind off Jerusalem   43
My Mother: 33 years later   44
On the Bank Street Pier   46
no love   47
What has happened?   48
We quarreled   49

Question   50

Old Age Porch   51

Against darkness   52

For My Friend Who Planted A Tree For His Daughter Jane   53

THETFORD POEMS

   What would happen   55

   What is this whiteness   56

   When the wild strawberry

   In deepest summer   57

   St Johnswort

   A bee!   An ant!   58

   Then the flowers became very wild   59

   I don't think   60

SOME NEARLY SONGS

   The Old Dog's Song   61

   34th Street Song   62

   The Sad Children's Song   63

III   *He travels three hundred miles to New York*   66

Standing in high grass at home   67

Quarrel   68

My Father at 85   69

My Father at 89   70

Oh the Dreamer said   71

On the Subway Station   72

Connections: Vermont   Vietnam (I)   73

Two Villages   74

Connections: Vermont   Vietnam (II)   76

This is about the women of that country   78

Illegal Aliens   80

If you have acquired a taste for happiness   81

Definition   82

Now time himself, the master streamer   83

That Year   84

Afterword by Jane Cooper   87

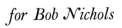

for Bob Nichols

I

A woman invented fire and called it
                    the wheel
Was it because the sun is round
          I saw the round sun bleeding to sky
And fire rolls across the field
          from forest to treetop
It leaps like a bike with a wild boy riding it

oh   she said
          see the orange wheel of heat
light that took me from the
          window of my mother's home
to home in the evening

Stanzas: Old Age and the Conventions of Retirement
Have Driven My Friends from the Work They Love

1

When she was young she wanted
to sing in a bank
a song about money
　　　　　the lyrics of gold
was her song
　　　　　she dressed for it

2

She did good. She stood up like a
planted flower among yellow weeds
　　　　　turning to please the sun
　　　　　they were all shiny
it was known she was planted

3

No metaphor reinvents the job of the nurture of children
except to muddy or mock.

4

the job of hunting of shooting in hunting season of
standing alone in the woods of being an Indian

5

The municipal center
the morning of anger
the centrifugal dream
her voice flung out on plates of rage
    then they were put in a paper sack
    she was sent to the china closet
    and never came back

6

Every day he went out, forsaking
wife and child
with his black bag he accompanied
the needle of pain as it
sewed our lives to death

7

One day at work   he cried
I am in my full powers
    suddenly he was blind
when slabs of time and aperture returned
dear friend   we asked
    what do you see
he said   I only see what has been
    seen already

One day when I was a child   long ago
Mr. Long Ago spoke up in school
He said
Oh children you must roll your r's
no no not on your tongue little girl
IN YOUR THROAT
there is nothing so beautiful as r rolled in the throat of a French woman
no woman more beautiful
he said   looking back
                    back
                    at beauty

Drowning (I)

If I were in the middle of the Atlantic
        drowning   far from home
I would look up at the sky
        veil of my hiding life
and say:
        goodbye

then I would sink

the second time I'd come up   I'd say:
        these are the willful waves of the watery sea
        which is drowning me
then I would sink
the third time I'd come up: it would be my last
        my arms   reaching
        my knees   falling
I'd cry   oh   oh
        first friend of my thinking head
        dear flesh
        farewell

Drowning (II)

This is how come I am drowned:
    First the sun shone on me
    Then the wind blew over me
    Then the sand polished me
    Then the sea touched me
    Then the tide came

The women let the tide go out
                    which will return which will return
the sand, the salt, the fat drowned babies
The men ran furiously
                along the banks of the estuary
screaming
         Come back you fucking sea
right now
         right now

A Warning

One day I forgot Jerusalem and my right arm is withered
My right arm, my moving arm, my rising and falling arm
                    my loving arm
Is withered

And my left eye, the blinker and winker is plucked out
It hangs by six threads of endless remembering.
Because I forgot Jerusalem
And wherever I go, I am known, I am recognized at once. I am
                    perceived by strangers.
Because on one day, only one day I forgot Jerusalem.

Jews everywhere, Jews, old deaths of the north and south
                    kingdoms,
Poor Jews in the ghetto walls built by the noble slav,
                    Jew princes
In Amsterdam who live in diamond houses that shine like window
                    panes
Listen to me. Wherever you go, keep the nation of that city
                    in mind
For I forgot her and now I am blind and crippled.

Even my lover, a Christian with pale eyes and the barbarian's foreskin
                    has left me.

The veins that stand on the back of my sunburned hand
are something like the branched veins on the flat tan
                         shore of the bay
Out of these, when the tide tugs
salt sea runs   back
into the rocky basin from which
we came
on the first day   specks
in a stranded pool   dashed
in high tide   alive
on the hot dry land.

At the Battery

I am standing on one foot
at the prow of great Manhattan
leaning forward
projecting a little into the bright harbor

If only a topographer in a helicopter
would pass over my shadow
I might be imposed forever
on the maps of this city

20th Street   Spring

the wives of the black-sailed seminarians
take their children to walk with green pails

they are light-haired and slim   their husbands are studying
passion and service   the seminary

is old the baby leaves of the old sycamores are pale green
are river yellow like the high light arms of the sycamore

the seminary is red and soot-darkened
by the soot-making city   it is at the side of the city near the river

it stands aside from the piers and the warehouses and the longshoremen
it intends to be quiet and dark   though sunlight surrounds it

sun lies on the streets and the lawns and the children
of the seminarians play with red hoops in the street in the sun

note to grandparents

the children are healthy
    the children are rosy
we take them to the park
    we take them to the playground

they swing on the swings
    the wind smacks their faces
they jump and are lively
    they eat everything

they sleep without crying
    they are very smart
each day they grow
    you would hardly know them

psalm

their shoes are stuccoed with sawdust and blood
the two young butchers walk singing together on ninth avenue
the sun is out because it is the lunch hour
they kick the melting snow and splash into deep puddles
then they embrace one another in the cold air
for water and singing may wash away the blood of the lamb

Mulberry Street ends in good works
The Committee for Nonviolent Action begins there
Also St. Barnabas House which shelters abandoned children

And on the corner of Mott Street
Bob Nichols is making a playground
single-handed   two mountains   an iron tower from which
the cliffs of Houston Street can be observed
a maple glade   a ship at sea

The boys from St. Bernard's
and the boys from
Our Lady of Pompeii
converge on the corner of Bleecker and Bank

There is a grinding of snowballs
and a creaking of ice

The name of our Lord is invoked

But for such healthy tough warriors
He has other deaths in mind

Sulky
They part

Children walking with their grandmothers
talk foreign languages
that is the nature of this city
and also this country

Talk is cheap but comes in variety
and witnessing dialect
there is a rule for all
and in each sentence a perfect grammar

On the Fourth Floor

The woman on the fourth floor said You slut! don't you knock on my
           door   stand up straight   be a woman!
The girl said   I ain't a slut   I didn't have no father   my mother. . .
The woman said   Stop that   neither did I   I didn't have nothin
The girl said I ain't a slut   I don't fuck guys
The woman said   Who cares about guys you're disgusting   you ain't
           a woman
You're dirty look at you you can't keep your eyes open

The boy came to the head of the stairs He hollered   Diana come up
           here   where's the tuinals
The girl said I ain't got them
The boy screamed   I had sixteen   I ate ten   I give you four   there's
           two left someplace
I ain't got them   I only got two methodone
Look at you   the boy said   you hung down to the ground   you ate them
I didn't   she said come with me Eddie
to the East River Drive   There's a party I'll say you're my husband
The boy screamed   get me the two tuinal

The woman took the girl's hand Go into your house   right this
           minute   pay him no mind
wash up   you stink   comb your hair   straight yourself
ain't you ashamed? Be a woman

Middle Age Poem

          With what joy
I left home to deposit one thousand, one hundred and nineteen
          dollars in the bank
I was whistling and skipping
you would think I had a new baby and a new cradle
after so many years
or that my mother had come to visit from Queens, borough of
          cemeteries
you would think a lover
was waiting
at the corner of Chemical Trust
and First National
right under the willow oak
with open arms

On Mother's Day

I went out walking
in the old neighborhood

Look! more trees on the block
forget-me-nots all around them
ivy   lantana shining
and geraniums in the window

Twenty years ago
it was believed that the roots of trees
would insert themselves into gas lines
then fall   poisoned on houses and children

or tap the city's water pipes
or starved for nitrogen   obstruct the sewers

In those days in the afternoon I floated
by ferry to Hoboken or Staten Island
then pushed the babies in their carriages
along the river wall   observing Manhattan
See Manhattan I cried   New York!
even at sunset it doesn't shine
but stands in fire   charcoal to the waist

But this Sunday afternoon on Mother's Day
I walked west   and came to Hudson Street   tri-colored flags
were flying over old oak furniture for sale
brass bedsteads   copper pots and vases
by the pound from India

Suddenly before my eyes   twenty-two transvestites
in joyous parade stuffed pillows
under their lovely gowns
and entered a restaurant
under a sign which said   All Pregnant Mothers Free

I watched them place napkins over their bellies
and accept coffee and zabaglione

I am especially open to sadness and hilarity
since my father died as a child
one week ago in this his ninetieth year

Having Arrived by Bike at Battery Park

I thought I would
sit down at one of those park department tables
and write a poem honoring
the occasion which is May 25th
Evelyn   my best friend's birthday
and Willy Langbauer's birthday

Day! I love you for your delicacy
in appearing after so many years
as an afternoon in Battery Park right
on the curved water
where Manhattan was beached

At once arrows
straight as Broadway were driven
into the great Indian heart

Then we came from the east
seasick and safe the
white tormented people
grew fat in the
blood of that wound

II

A stranger calling a dog whistled
and I came running though I am not an afghan

or a highclass poodle and not much like a
city boy's dog with a happy wild tail and red eyes

The stranger said excuse me, I was calling my dog not you
Ah   I replied   to this courteous explanation

Sometimes I whistle too   but mostly for fear
of missing the world I am a dog to whistlers

on certain days I am not in love
and my heart turns over

       crowding the lungs for
       air

       driving blood in and out of
       the skull   improving my mind

       working muscles to the bone

       dashing resonance out of a roaring sea
       at my nerve endings

not much is needed

       air

       good sense

       power

       a noisy taking in and a
       loud giving back

then my heart like any properly turned

motor   takes off in sparks dragging all that machinery
through the blazing day
       like grass
             which our lord knows
        I am

One day lying on my stomach in the afternoon trying to sleep
I suffered penis envy (much to
                          my surprise

and with no belief in Freud   for years
                          in fact   extreme
antipathy)   what could I do but turn around

and close my eyes and dream of summer
                          in those days I
                          was a boy I whistled
at the gate for Tom

Then I woke up
then I slept
and dreamed another dream

in my drowned father's empty pocket
there were nine dollars and the salty sea
  he said   I know you   my darling girl
you're the one that's me

Some days I am lonesome   I want to talk to my mother
And she isn't home
Then I ask my father   Where has she been the last twenty years?
And he answers
Where do you think you fool as usual?
> She is asleep in Abraham's bosom
> Resting from years of your incessant provocation
> Exhausted by infinite love of me
> Escaping from the boredom of days shortening to Christmas
> and the pain of days lengthening to Easter
> You know where she is   She is at ease in Zion with all
> the other dead Jews

I cannot keep my mind on Jerusalem
It wanders off like an idiot with no attention span
to whatever city lies outside my window that day
      Damascus
         the libraries of Babylonia
Oh! the five exogamous boroughs of
our beloved home New York

What will happen
when the Lord
remembers vengeance
(which is his)
and finds me

My Mother: 33 years later

                    1
There are places
    garden
    music room
    stove
    dining room

death bed   her eyes are open   she doesn't speak
    my sister and I hold up a picture of Frannie the first grandchild
    Mama do you know who this is?
    Fools! Who do you think you're talking to?
    Oh! she cried and turned away

my room   she says
    I've heard that expression
    I know how you talk
    don't think I'm so dumb
    hot pants! that's what you say, you girls!

Bobby and I are walking, arm in arm, across the campfield
Our mothers are behind us. We're nine years old.
We're wearing swimming trunks.
                                    She says
    look see the line of soft soft
    hair along their spines
    like down   our little birds

One of the mothers
the mother out of whose body
I easily appeared

Once I remembered her

2

This is what I planned:
To get to the end of our life quickly

And begin again

Everyone is intact   talking
Mother and Father   Mira   Babashka
all of us eating our boiled egg
but the poplar tree on Hoe Avenue
has just been cut down and the Norway maple
is planted in Mahopac

Then
my mother gives me
a vase full of zinnias
"as straight as little Russian Soldiers"

yes
mama
as straight as the second grade
in the P.S. 50 school yard
at absolute attention
under its woolen hats
of pink   orange   lavender   yellow

On the Bank Street Pier

In the mind's eye
    the mind cries I I I
the mother's face
    the father's looking eye
then sees
    then says
the scrambled iron piers
    the river's broad as
    mother's face

In the mind's ear
    talk talk talk
    the tickling tongue
of strangers

no love
    no love cried the last fling
        in the vase
        on the piano
no love
    her dress like a garden
        her knees
        in the water

her dress
    white peacocks with green tails

is that beautiful she said
            beautiful he said
            touching the marigold's dust

What has happened?
language eludes me
the nice   specifying
words of my life fail
when I call

Ah says a friend
dried up no doubt
on the dessicated
twigs in the swamp
of the skull like
a lake where the
waterlevel has been
shifted by highways
a couple of miles off

Another friend says
No no My dear   perhaps
you are only meant to
speak more plainly

We quarreled
Alone I
turned away
from her dear
face then I
feared death

Question

Do you think old people should be put away
the one red rheumy eye   the pupil that goes back and back
the hands are scaly
                    do you think all that should be hidden

do you think young people should be seen so much on Saturday nights
hunting and singing in packs the way they do
standing on street corners looking this way and that

or the small children who are visible all the time everywhere
and have nothing to do but be smart
but be athletes
but jump
but climb high fences
                    do you think hearts should sink
                    do you think the arteries ought to crumble
                    when they could do good?
because the heart was made to endure
                    why does it not endure?
                    do you think this is the way it should be?

Old Age Porch

All morning they store suns
against the grave
            but this is useless
if you have ever seen a dead person
            you know it

Your friend lies in darkness   all
that sunlight spilled around her
in the watery rays you make a song
you invent the days
            of friendship

Against darkness
I send money
to the American
Federation
for the Blind

Not to be spared
pain   but for grappling
nerve when I come
out of all arrival to
the departure of senses

For My Friend Who Planted a Tree for His Daughter Jane

Up here we don't plant trees   sometimes we take them down
we want to give back the cleared land   the farmers' hard work long ago

Because the forest moves easily on its red sumach and wild cherry toes
and near the pond the alder and willow stretch toward the tall reeds

They hold the swamp in place for a few years
then they lie down themselves and thicken the earth

So I have looked for a standing tree to call it
                                        Jane

lovely child of my beloved friend   apple tree planted
one year ago   I think you are Jane's tree

apple tree of earliest apples   apple tree of
the summer farmer who sees winter only once in awhile

In the cleared field you stand   hemlock and pine
not too far off   and the birch tree   familiar

as the face of our Russian grandparents   white
as their friendly ghosts   I will say   Jane   in August

when the pale apples are ready   then we return
the core to earth   after frost the late apples

redden   grow tart with time and the cold nights   we look west
toward the valley villages   the small orchard   the fruit

early and late tumbled under light snow
sweet mulch of this sweet earth

What would happen
if there were a terrific shortage of goldenrod
in the world
and I put my foot outside this house
to walk in my garden and show city visitors
my two lovely rosebushes
and three remarkable goldenrod plants
that were doing well this year

I would say: Look!
how on each of several sprigs
there are two three dozen tiny stems
and on each stem three four tiny golden
flowers   petals stamen pistil and the pollen
which bees love
                    but insufficiently
otherwise
            can you imagine the fields
on rainy days in August   brass
streaking the lodged hayheads
dull brass in the rain
and under the hot sun
the golden flowers
            floating   gold dust of August fields
for miles and miles

what is this whiteness on the fields?
                    not rime
nor the Lord's snowy reason for exploding summer
it is the mist
                    that starts the day
with drinks for all

When the wild strawberry leaves turn
red and show the dark place of the strawberries
it is too late

I know this has a
meaning inside my own life
inside dark life

In deepest summer
the milkweed flower
dries to pod   in autumn
flies like seed and dies
in earth and is reborn

but not until
disaster strikes the field
and lays the grasses down
under the weighty ice
in which the water lives

St Johnswort

it must be summertime
buttercup   gone
hawkweed   gone

black eyed susan
            before you
know it   queen anne's lace

goldenrod and that
will be that

A bee!
drowning in
a wild rose
    flat on its
    round back
    kicking
too young to
use love for
health and
enrichment

An ant!
lugging half an ounce
of carcass across
the cement porch steps
    he's lost
    he struggled back and forth
    he carries a feast
    for his family
We can't find them
we looked under the steps
there wasn't a stray nation
anywhere

Then the flowers became very wild
because it was early September
and they had nothing to lose
they tossed their colors every
which way over the garden wall
splattering the lawn shoving their
wild orange red rain-disheveled faces
into my window without shame

I don't think
the rain will end
today   this is
because I come
from another
country

The Old Dog's Song

Where can I shit
            said the old dog
turning this way and that
the grasses are gone
                  the asphalt is slimy with oil
on the nice rubbly lots
                  there are six story buildings
where can I shit
            said the old dog
            turning this way and that

Where can I turn
            said the old dog
no one is in heat
                  on this block at least
my old friends have altered
      or snap   they show me their teeth
                  not their ass
            said the old dog
turning this way and that

This leash is so loose
                  said the old dog
turning this way and that
nobody cares if I run
                  the children have gone
the man who hangs on is like me
he looks up the block and then down
                  turning this way and that
said the old dog
                  turning this way and that

61

34th Street Song

With joy she showed the traveller Macy's
That's Macy's there   right by Korvette's
                                   and Gimbels

Oh you were right not to get out at 14th Street
May's is nice but Klein's was the store
                                   and it ended

The Sad Children's Song

This house is a wreck said the children
when they came home with their children
Your papers are all over the place
The chairs are covered with books
and look brown leaves are piled on the floor
under the wandering Jews

Your face is a wreck said the children
when they came home with their children
There are lines all over your face
your necks like curious turtles
Why did you let yourself go?
Where are you going without us?

This world is a wreck said the children
When they came home with their children
There are bombs all over the place
There's no water the fields are all poisoned
Why did you leave things like this
Where can we go said the children
what can we say to our children?

III

He travels three hundred miles to New York
carrying all the works of Kawabata
when he returns he brings them back with him

What are they doing in his suitcase all that time

Speaking to one another as the books of any author will do
arguing the past and future of technical authority
ghosts invented for melody's sake Its the tune
the time sings   all our stories are set to it

Sitting in the bus   watching New England curl
around its rivers   thinking of his own long
difficult novel he will place THE SOUND
OF THE MOUNTAIN on his lap   he will ask
its intelligent advice

Standing in high grass at home imagining farm
    and granary   he looks east
                he praises Him
                astonished
and last night as we returned from our long walk
across Luquillo Beach we saw the colorless sun fall
between dark rain and the flashing sea
                        I think he praised Him
white birds flew up against the night
But for everyday life, he shows no gratitude

Still his courage is greater than mine
Days pass   No voice answers his
                  My dear I say
this is because the times are bad
speaker and speaker do not know one another
and the song sung by the people to the singer
is not known
            though the melody is theirs

Quarrel

Bob and I
    in different rooms
    talking to ourselves
carrying on
    last night's
    hard conversation
convinced
    the other one
    the life companion
    wasn't listening

My Father at 85

My father said
> how will they get out of it
> they're sorry they got in

My Father says
> how will they get out
> Nixon Johnson   the whole bunch
> they don't know how

goddamit he says
> I'd give anything to see it
> they went in over their heads

he says
> greed   greed   time
> nothing is happening fast enough

My Father at 89

His brain simplified itself
saddening everyone   but he
asked us   children
don't you remember my dog Mars
who met me on the road
when I came home   lonesome
and singing   walking
from the Czar's prison

Oh the dreamer said
and dreamed himself she

it was an unusual day
when all the suns stood
visible and we could see
our light small sighted sun

its rays were bones
of the old wars

On the Subway Station

The child is speaking to the father
he is looking into the father's eyes
father doesn't answer
child is speaking Vietnamese
father doesn't answer
child is speaking English
father doesn't answer
The father is staring at a mosaic in blue and green
and lavender   three small ships in harbor
set again and again in the white tiled
beautiful   old   unrenovated subway
station   Clark Street   Brooklyn

Connections: *Vermont Vietnam* (I)

Hot summer day
on the River Road
swimmers of the Ompompanoosuc
dust in my eyes
       oh
       it is the hot wind from Laos
       the girl in Nhe An covers her face with a straw hat
       as we pass   she breathes   through cloth
       she stands between two piles of stone

       the dust of National Highway One blinds

me
summertime
I drive through Vermont
my fist on the horn, barefoot
      like Ching

Two Villages

In Duc Ninh a village of 1,654 households
Over 100 tons of rice and casava were burned
18,138 cubic meters of dyke were destroyed
There were 1077 air attacks
There is a bomb crater that measures 150 feet across
It is 50 feet deep

Mr. Tat said: The land is more exhausted than the people
                        I mean to say that the poor earth
                        is tossed about
                        thrown into the air again and again
                        it knows no rest

                        whereas the people have dug tunnels
                        and trenches   they are able in this way
                        to lead normal family lives

            In Trung Trach
a village of 850 households
a chart is hung in the House of Tradition

rockets   522
attacks   1201
big bombs   6998
napalm   1383
time bombs   267
shells   12291
pellet bombs   2213

Mr. Tuong of the Fatherland Front
has a little book
in it he keeps the facts
carefully added

Connections: *Vermont   Vietnam* (II)

The generals came to the president
We are the laughing stock of the world
What world? he said

> the world
> the world

Vermont
  the green world
  the green mountain

Across the valley
someone is clearing a field
he is making a tan rectangle
he has cut a tan rectangle on Lyme   Hill
the dark wood
the deposed farm

> the mist is sipped up by the sun
> the mist is eaten by the sun

What world? he said

What mountain? said the 20 ships of the Seventh Fleet
rolling on the warm waves lobbing shells all the summer day
into green distance

on Trung Son Mountain Phan Su told a joke:
The mountain is torn, the trees are broken
How easy it is to gather wood
to repair my house in the village which is broken by bombs.

His shirt is plum-colored, is brown like dark plums
the sails on the sampans that fish in the sea of the Seventh Fleet
                    are plum-colored
the holes in the mountain are red
the earth of that province is red   red
                                        world

This is about the women of that country
sometimes they spoke in slogans
They said
    We patch the roads as we patch our sweetheart's trousers
    The heart will stop but not the transport
They said
    We have ensured production even near bomb craters
    Children let your voices sing higher than the explosions
                                of the bombs
They said
    We have important tasks to teach the children
    that the people are the collective masters
    to bear hardship
    to instill love in the family
    to guide for good health of the children (they must
    wear clothing according to climate)
They said
    once men beat their wives
    now they may not
    once a poor family sold its daughter to a rich old man
    now the young may love one another
They said
    once we planted our rice any old way
    now we plant the young shoots in straight rows
    so the imperialist pilot can see how steady our
    hands are

In the evening we walked along the shores of the Lake
                            of the Restored Sword

I said   is it true? we are sisters?
They said, Yes, we are of one family

Illegal Aliens

The Chicago Airport
O'Hare
4:30 A.M.

fifty men
in double lines
handcuffed

dark men

probably Mexicans
wearing
the work clothes

in which they were taken

brightness of the airport
the empty shopping stalls blaze

a tall sandy-haired man
leads them not in uniform
gray pants an ordinary
windbreaker   he calls
aquí   aquí   waving his hands

a young woman in the rear
shouts   go on now
aquí aquí you got to
go the way he says

If you have acquired a taste for happiness
                it's very hard to do without
so you try jollity for awhile
jokes
        and
                merriment

Song is one of the famous methods
for continuing or entrenching
                                happiness

Here is another example of ordinary joy:
                the gathering together of comrades
                in disagreement and resolution
                followed by determined action

Still   the face of life will change
partly because of those miserable scratches it makes
on its own aging surface
                        Then
                        happiness

in the risky busy labor of Repair the World
after which   for the unsated   there will surely be
talking all night   dances in schoolrooms and kitchens
                        and sometimes
                        love
of happinesses   the most famous of all

Definition

My dissent is cheer
a thankless disposition
first as the morning star
    my ambition: good luck

and why not   a flight
over the wide dilemna
and then good night to
    sad forever

Now time himself   the master streamer
grew
by pools and ponds
then strenuously   to accomodate the generations
became a sea

In which the fish and thee
my love   by dark and night light swim
and nations drown

That Year

In my family
people who were eighty-two were very different
from people who were ninety-two

The eighty-two year old people grew up
          it was 1914
          this is what they knew
          War   World War   War

That's why when they speak to the child
they say
          poor little one. . .

The ninety-two year old people remember
          it was the year 1905
          they went to prison
          they went into exile
          they said   ah   soon

When they speak to the grandchild
they say
          yes   there will be revolution
          then there will be revolution   then
          once more   then the earth itself
          will turn and turn and cry out   oh I
          have been made sick

                    then you   my little bud
                         must flower and save it

AFTERWORD

Before, during, and after writing her stories, Grace Paley has always been a poet. She has a theory of the two languages. All writers, she holds, all children as they learn to speak, inherit both the gorgeous language stored up for them in books and the first, crooning or combative language of the bedroom and the street. She loves to read Milton out loud with her students. She loves kitchens, markets, fairs, political demonstrations, any gathering where people open up their mouths to get the day's work done. Then there is a third language probably— whatever was heard by the child from immigrant parents or grandparents, the ghosts of another rhythm and culture, in her case, Russian and Jewish.

When *The Little Disturbances of Man* came out, it was recognized that hers was a unique voice. Almost more than to the stories told, we listened to the teller. In *Enormous Changes at the Last Minute* and, most recently, *Later the Same Day*, it became clear that what had been discovered in sentences and paragraphs was being extended to the whole story form. Somehow, here was a new mix of concentration and openness. Can one still speak of "voice" when what is being referred to is a wit that could finish off a topic in a line or two were it not for the stubborn heart that insists the topic, the character, the human dilemma, be given another chance? Well, why not? Such a voice is the actual theme of "A Conversation with My Father," but it is implicit in the shape of many other stories Grace Paley has written.

I think not enough attention has been paid to her very brief tales, such as "A Conversation with My Father," "In This Country, But in Another Language, My Aunt Refuses to Marry the Men Everyone Wants Her To," and the one called simply "Mother." These tales are not like anyone else's; if they have a common ancestor (in another language) it is Chekhov. In two pages an entire history will be revealed. People move forward and back through time, in speculation. Little scenes blossom and disappear. To these tales the poems are most nearly related, having the same abrupt, often brilliant transitions and apparently candid speech.

But it would be a mistake to approach the poems as if they grew out of the tales. In fact, they are a kind of blue-print for them, and the tales are read most intelligently if one remembers that Paley wrote nothing but poems till she was almost thirty. Perhaps the poems represent some remaining shy or non-public side of her. Or they are conversations with herself about whatever she sees, suffers, invents, suddenly wants to point out in an access of delight, crying "Look! Look!" Or they are brief, truthful melodies that are the pure distillation of an instant's widest view. Most have never been published before. A few came out in magazines that have since gone out of business. We owe Granite Press a debt that we are holding this book in our hands.

What sort of book is it? The poems announce themselves wonderfully:

A woman invented fire and called it
the wheel

This is a new genesis, a feminist one, with a woman doing not only the creating but the naming, Adam's traditional task. She is in fact the first artist. And where does her art take her?

> . . . from the
>
> window of my mother's home
>
> to home in the evening

from the first home out of which at dawn the child stares hungrily toward experience to the last home she makes for herself at sundown: a day, a life, hummed disarmingly in a dozen lines.

Grace Paley is one of the most surprising, and satisfying, writers around. Immediately the poems confront aging, dying, the differences between women and men, the "healthy tough" lives of the young and children, who are her strong hope in the heartland of Lower Manhattan. Who else knows so well every tree that grows in the city? (Confucius said the job of poets is to teach us the names of plants, trees, and birds.) Who else can write so cheerfully about money and work? At the same time, the poems are full of mortal wisdom, a genuine tragic sense, such that we not only laugh at the comic vision of the "twenty-two transvestites" in "On Mother's Day" but laugh in a deeper way, with the poet, in grieving acknowledgment, because

> I am especially open to sadness and hilarity
>
> since my father died as a child
>
> one week ago in this his ninetieth year

All this is in Section I. The book is subtly and beautifully varied. Section II moves in a somewhat lighter, more inward vein and includes poems that celebrate the blooming summer countryside around Thetford, Vermont. Just at the end the old note of warning is struck, like a gong:

> This world is a wreck said the children . . .
>
> what can we say to our children?

Section III opens with poems about the lover and father, those two brave and responsible men, and then turns to Vietnam and so to poems, small and large, out of a lifetime's political consciousness. "My dissent is cheer," says one, "a thankless disposition"; while the last poem in the collection remembers the legacy of revolution for the sake of saving the earth brought over to this country by the "ninety-two year old people" from the Russia of 1905.

Given the state of the world in 1985, this is hardly a book that looks forward to immortality. Yet it is a wild, thoughtful, lyrical, honest, ultimately hopeful book. The writer in "He travels three hundred miles to New York" carries a Kawabata novel of which he asks "intelligent advice." And why shouldn't Grace Paley, as she dreams in "At the Battery,"

> . . . be imposed forever
> on the maps of this city

or at least for as long as the city is our garden and morning and evening home?

—Jane Cooper

BOOKS BY GRACE PALEY

LITTLE DISTURBANCES OF MAN
ENORMOUS CHANGES AT THE LAST MINUTE
LATER THE SAME DAY

Born in 1922, Grace Paley has lived in New York City most of her life. She has two grown children and a grandchild. She is married to Robert Nichols, a writer, and she lives with him in Vermont part of the year. She has called herself a combative pacifist and a cooperative anarchist and has always been active in anti-war and feminist causes. She teaches at Sarah Lawrence and City College.

With this title Granite Press enters trade publishing to expand distribution and widen exposure of essential writing by feminists and lesbians. The press has been operating as a letterpress printshop, designing jobs and publishing poetry chapbooks and broadsides by women since the early 70's. We plan to publish poetry and short stories and remain committed to clear and exciting book design. We welcome your support.